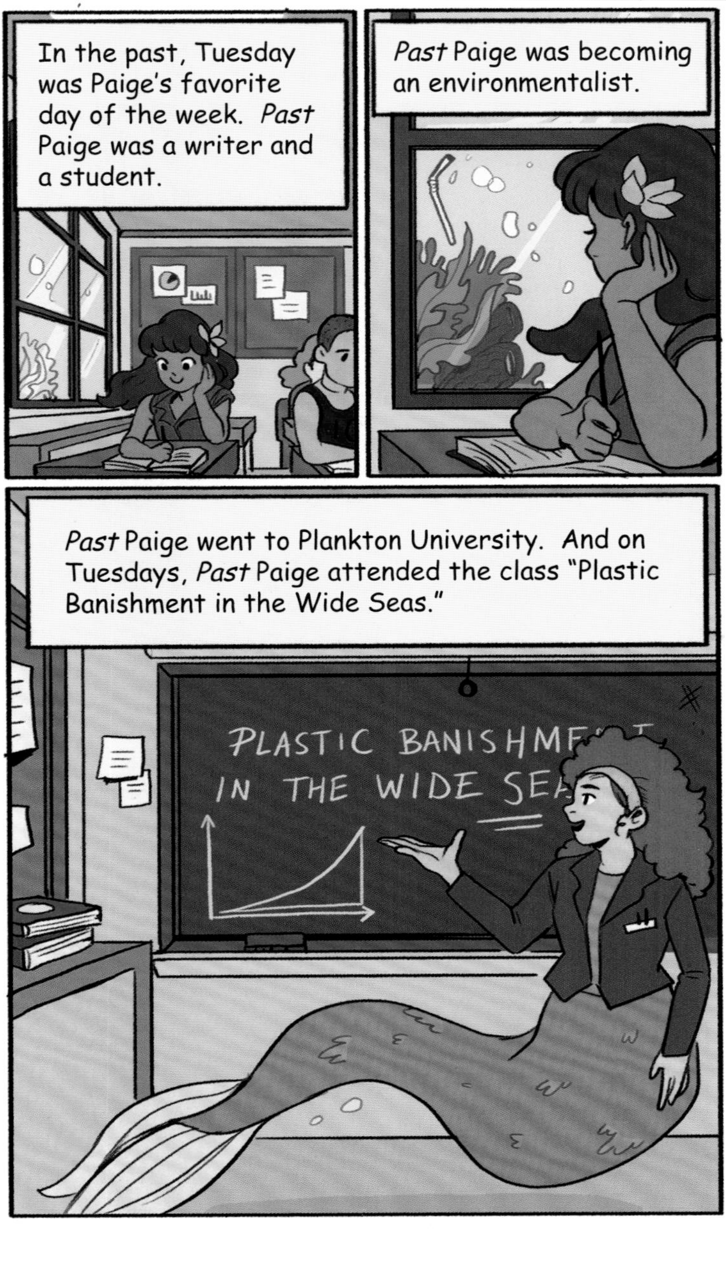
In the past, Tuesday was Paige's favorite day of the week. *Past* Paige was a writer and a student.
Past Paige was becoming an environmentalist.
Past Paige went to Plankton University. And on Tuesdays, *Past* Paige attended the class "Plastic Banishment in the Wide Seas."
PLASTIC
IN THE WIDE

She'd sit down in class with her 10 textbooks, all hand-me-downs from Polly, her older sister.

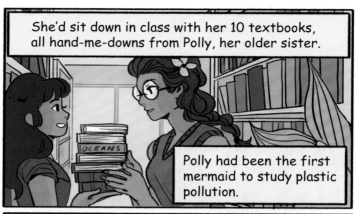

Polly had been the first mermaid to study plastic pollution.

On those Tuesdays of the past, Paige would write down how her marine friends were getting caught in plastic bags.

She'd examine where in the ocean the greatest number of plastic bottles were found.

PAIGE vs. PLASTIC

By Monika Davies
Illustrated by Arielle Jovellanos

Publishing Credits

Rachelle Cracchiolo, M.S.Ed., *Publisher*
Conni Medina, M.A.Ed., *Editor in Chief*
Nika Fabienke, Ed.D., *Content Director*
Véronique Bos, *Creative Director*
Shaun N. Bernadou, *Art Director*
Noelle Cristea, M.A.Ed., *Senior Editor*
John Leach, *Assistant Editor*
Jess Johnson, *Graphic Designer*

Image Credits

Illustrated by Arielle Jovellanos

Library of Congress Cataloging-in-Publication Data

Names: Davies, Monika, author. | Jovellanos, Arielle, illustrator.
Title: Paige vs. plastic / by Monika Davies ; illustrated by Arielle Jovellanos.
Other titles: Paige versus plastic
Description: Huntington Beach, CA : Teacher Created Materials, [2020] | Includes book club questions. | Audience: Age 10. | Audience: Grades 4-6.
Identifiers: LCCN 2019029962 (print) | LCCN 2019029963 (ebook) | ISBN 9781644913659 (paperback) | ISBN 9781644914557 (ebook)
Subjects: LCSH: Readers (Elementary) | Mermaids--Juvenile fiction. | Mermaids--Comic books, strips, etc. | Marine pollution--Juvenile fiction. | Marine pollution--Comic books, strips, etc. | Environmentalism--Juvenile fiction. | Environmentalsim--Comic books, strips, etc. | Graphic novels.
Classification: LCC PE1119 .D34685 2020 (print) | LCC PE1119 (ebook) | DDC 428.6/2--dc23
LC record available at https://lccn.loc.gov/2019029962
LC ebook record available at https://lccn.loc.gov/2019029963

TCM Teacher Created Materials
5301 Oceanus Drive
Huntington Beach, CA 92649-1030
www.tcmpub.com

ISBN 978-1-6449-1365-9

Table of Contents

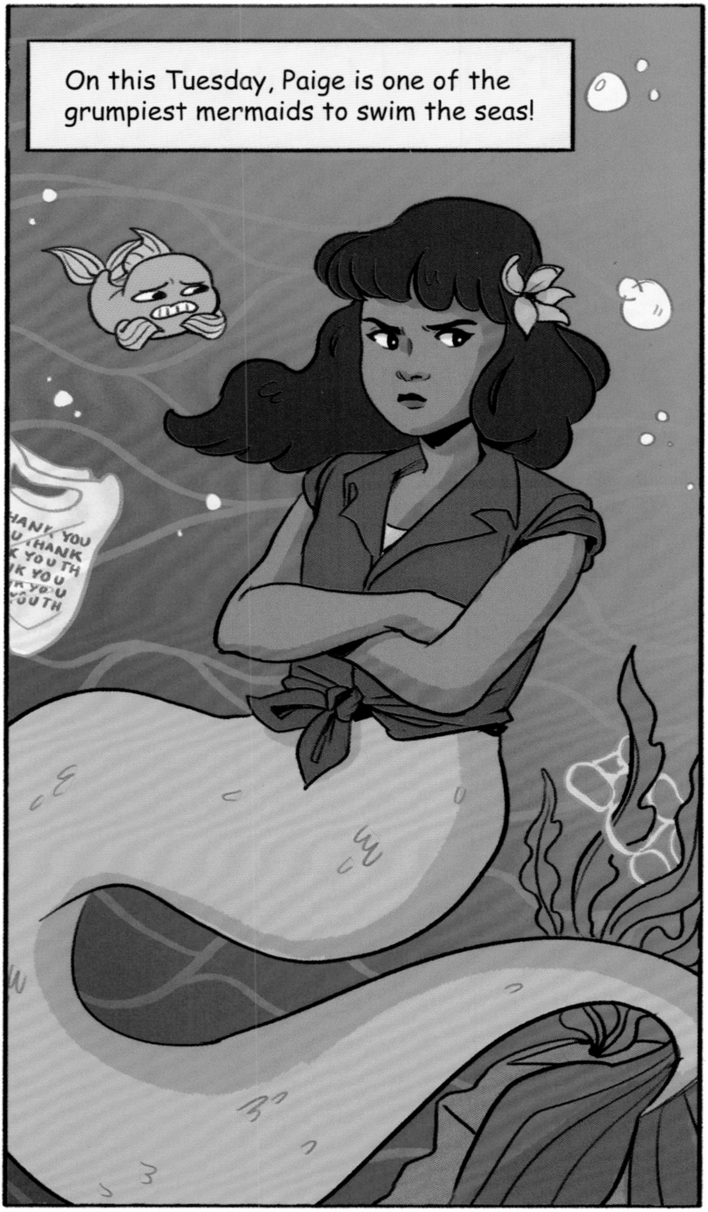
On this Tuesday, Paige is one of the grumpiest mermaids to swim the seas!

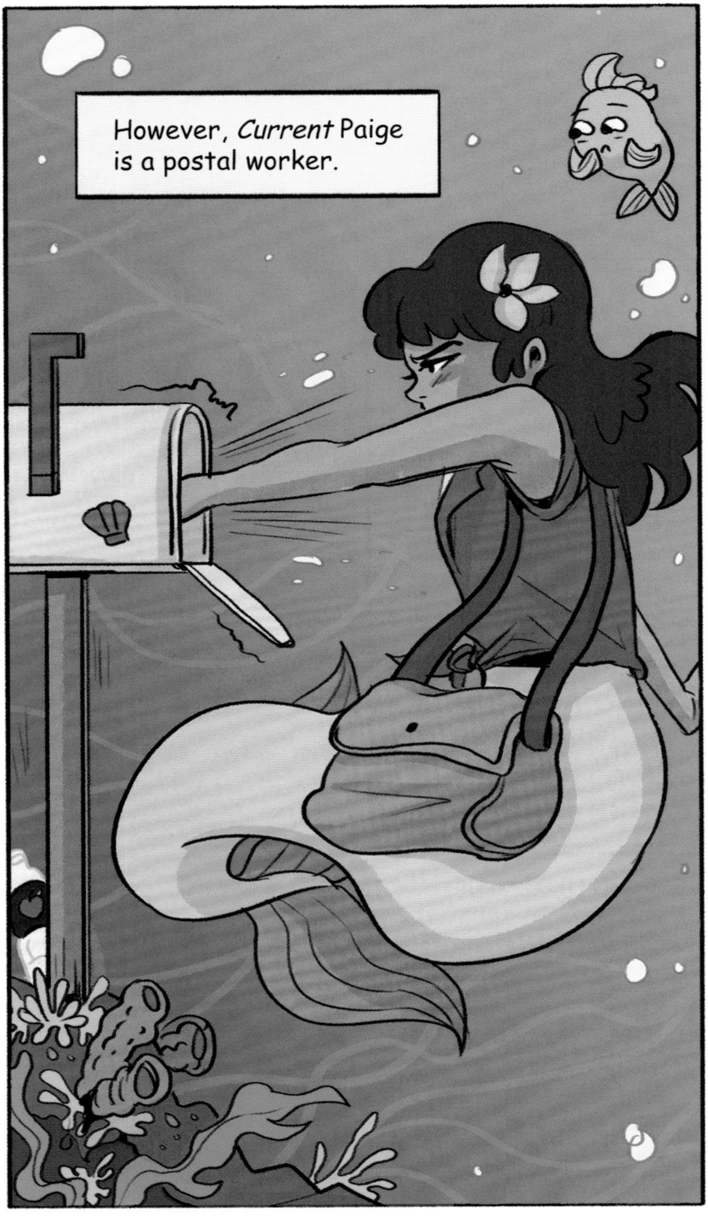
However, *Current* Paige is a postal worker.

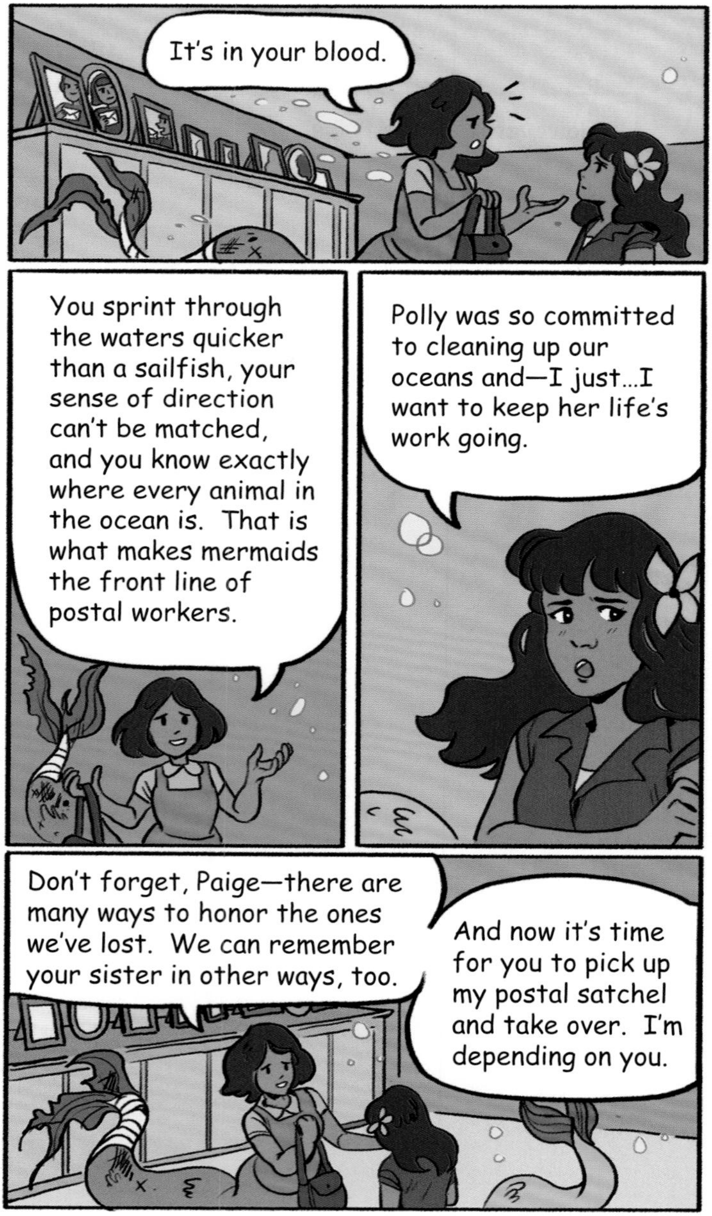
It's in your blood.
You sprint through the waters quicker than a sailfish, your sense of direction can't be matched, and you know exactly where every animal in the ocean is. That is what makes mermaids the front line of postal workers.
Polly was so committed to cleaning up our oceans and—I just...I want to keep her life's work going.
Don't forget, Paige—there are many ways to honor the ones we've lost. We can remember your sister in other ways, too.
And now it's time for you to pick up my postal satchel and take over. I'm depending on you.

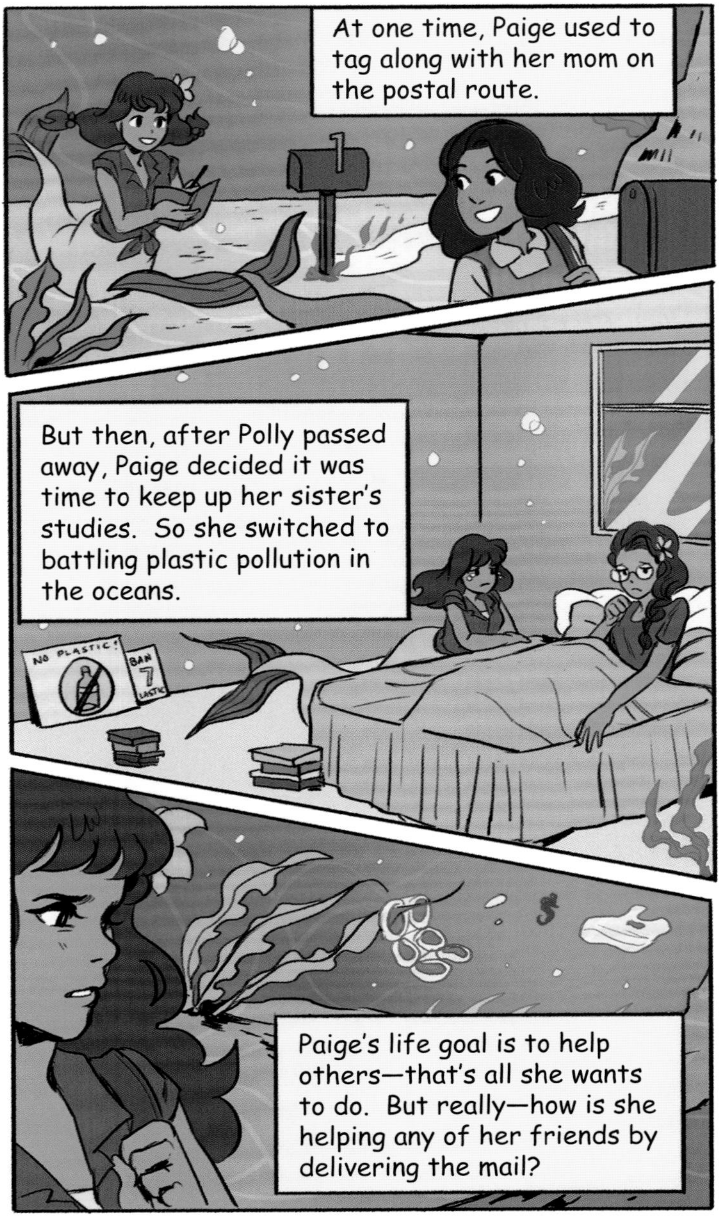
At one time, Paige used to tag along with her mom on the postal route.
But then, after Polly passed away, Paige decided it was time to keep up her sister's studies. So she switched to battling plastic pollution in the oceans.
NO PLASTIC!
BAN
Paige's life goal is to help others—that's all she wants to do. But really—how is she helping any of her friends by delivering the mail?

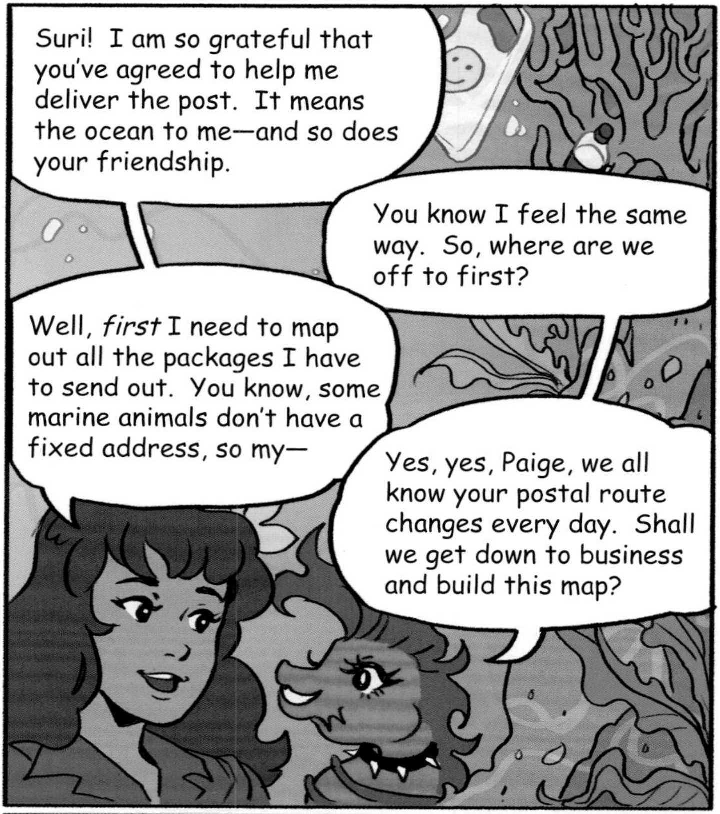
Suri! I am so grateful that you've agreed to help me deliver the post. It means the ocean to me—and so does your friendship.
You know I feel the same way. So, where are we off to first?
Well, *first* I need to map out all the packages I have to send out. You know, some marine animals don't have a fixed address, so my—
Yes, yes, Paige, we all know your postal route changes every day. Shall we get down to business and build this map?

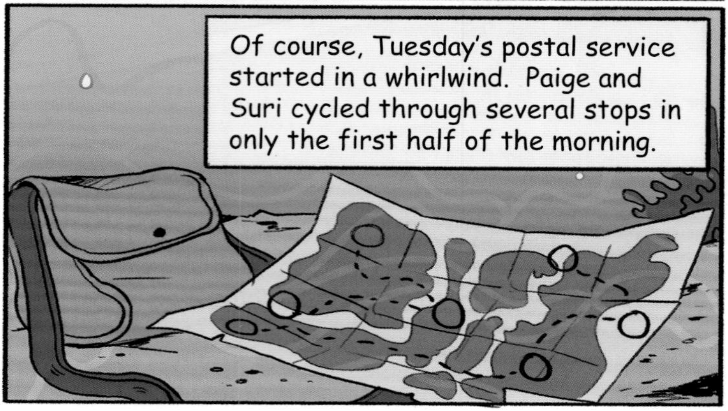
Of course, Tuesday's postal service started in a whirlwind. Paige and Suri cycled through several stops in only the first half of the morning.

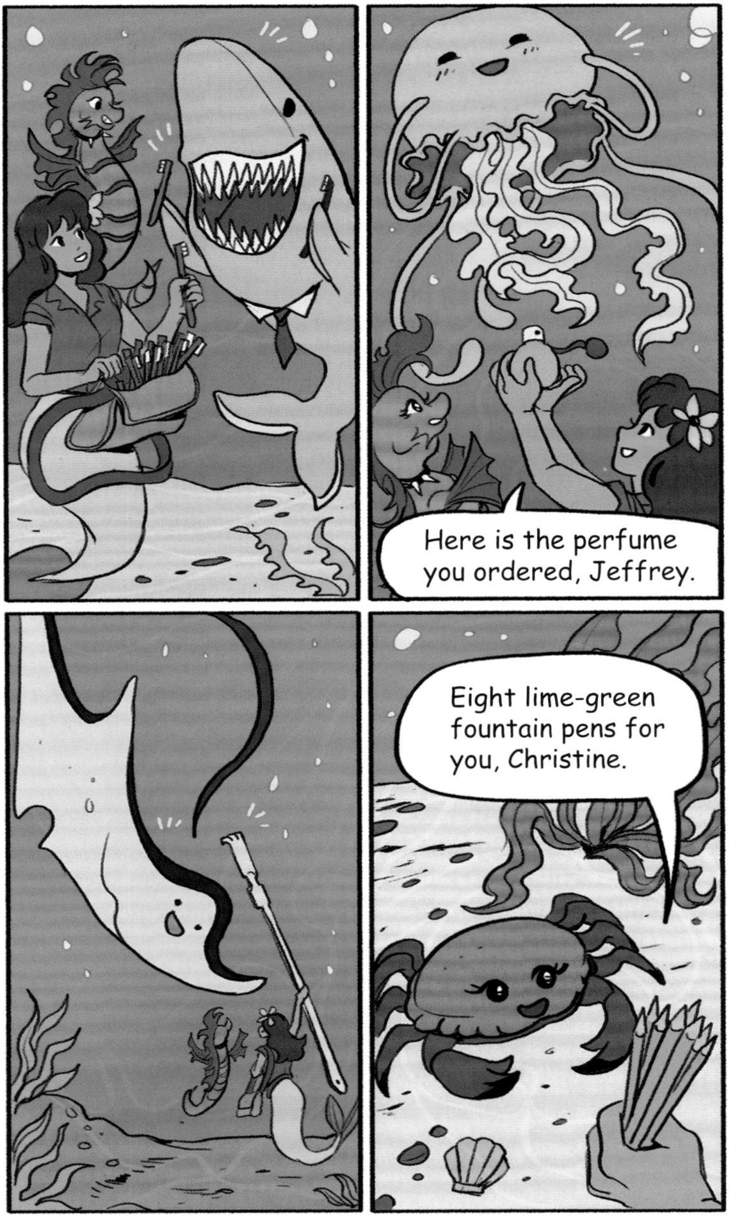
Here is the perfume you ordered, Jeffrey.
Eight lime-green fountain pens for you, Christine.

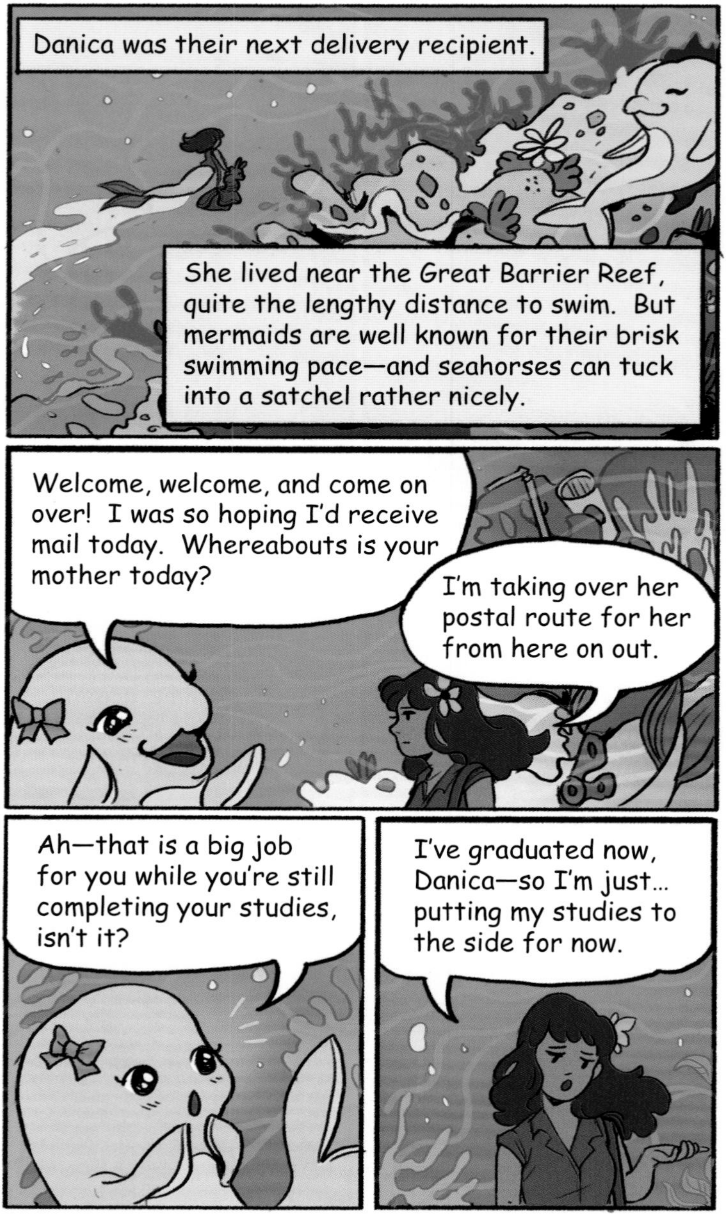
Danica was their next delivery recipient.
She lived near the Great Barrier Reef, quite the lengthy distance to swim. But mermaids are well known for their brisk swimming pace—and seahorses can tuck into a satchel rather nicely.
Welcome, welcome, and come on over! I was so hoping I'd receive mail today. Whereabouts is your mother today?
I'm taking over her postal route for her from here on out.
Ah—that is a big job for you while you're still completing your studies, isn't it?
I've graduated now, Danica—so I'm just... putting my studies to the side for now.

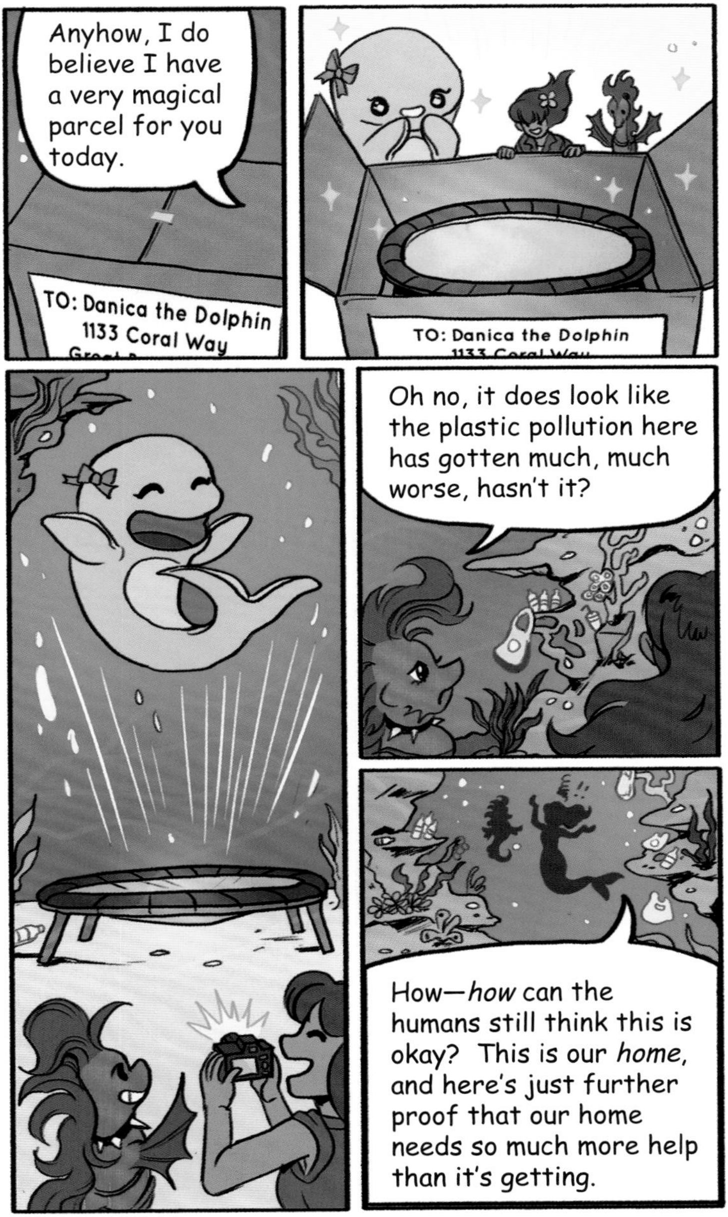
Anyhow, I do believe I have a very magical parcel for you today.
TO: Danica the Dolphin
1133 Coral Way
TO: Danica the Dolphin
Oh no, it does look like the plastic pollution here has gotten much, much worse, hasn't it?
How—*how* can the humans still think this is okay? This is our *home*, and here's just further proof that our home needs so much more help than it's getting.

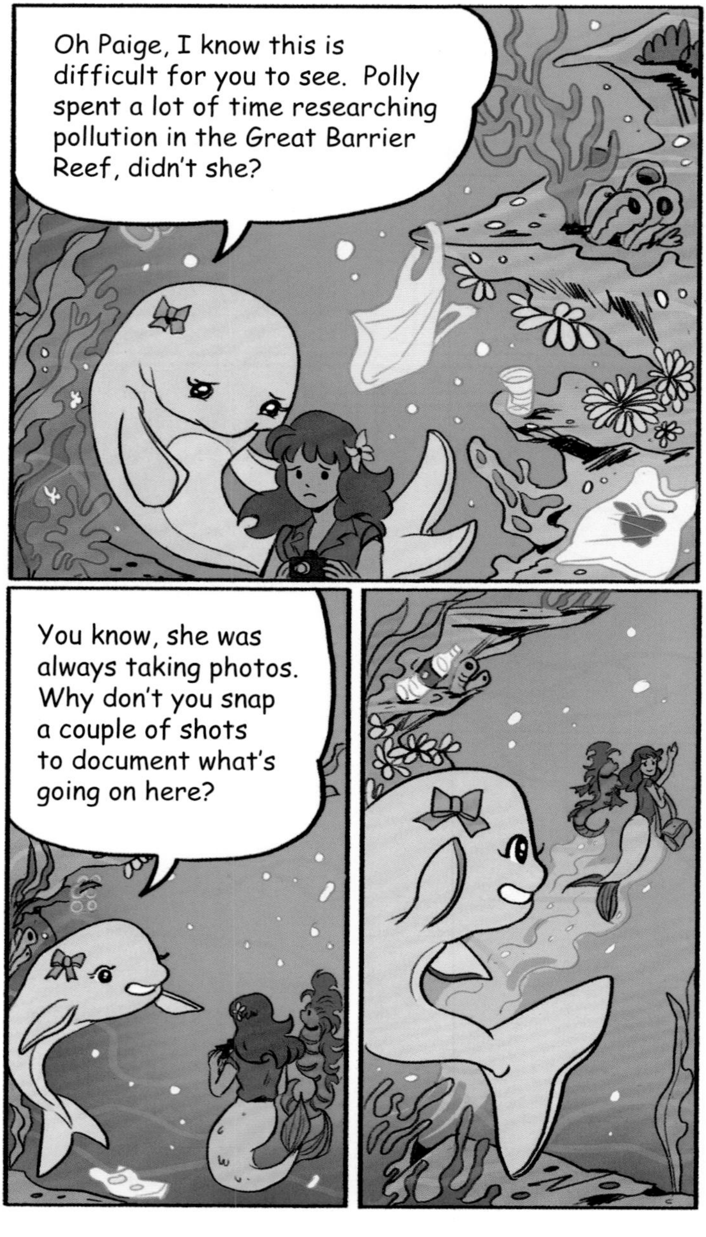
Oh Paige, I know this is difficult for you to see. Polly spent a lot of time researching pollution in the Great Barrier Reef, didn't she?
You know, she was always taking photos. Why don't you snap a couple of shots to document what's going on here?

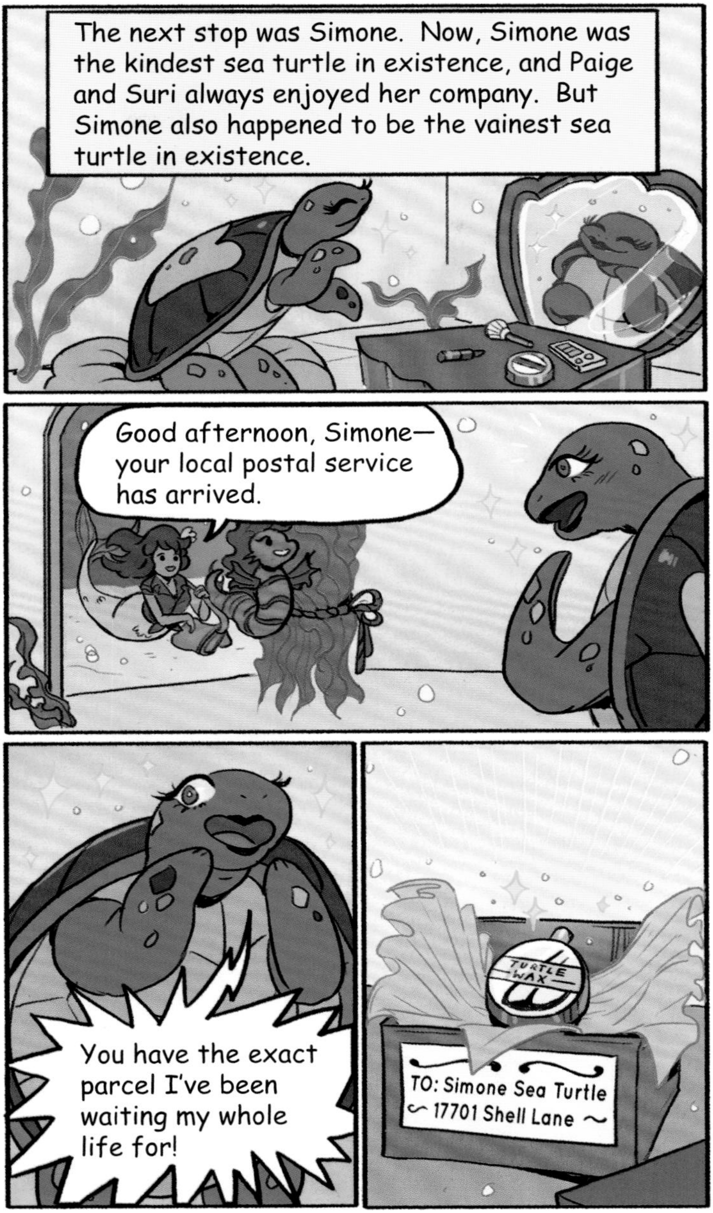
The next stop was Simone. Now, Simone was the kindest sea turtle in existence, and Paige and Suri always enjoyed her company. But Simone also happened to be the vainest sea turtle in existence.
Good afternoon, Simone— your local postal service has arrived.
You have the exact parcel I've been waiting my whole life for!
TURTLE WAX
TO: Simone Sea Turtle
17701 Shell Lane

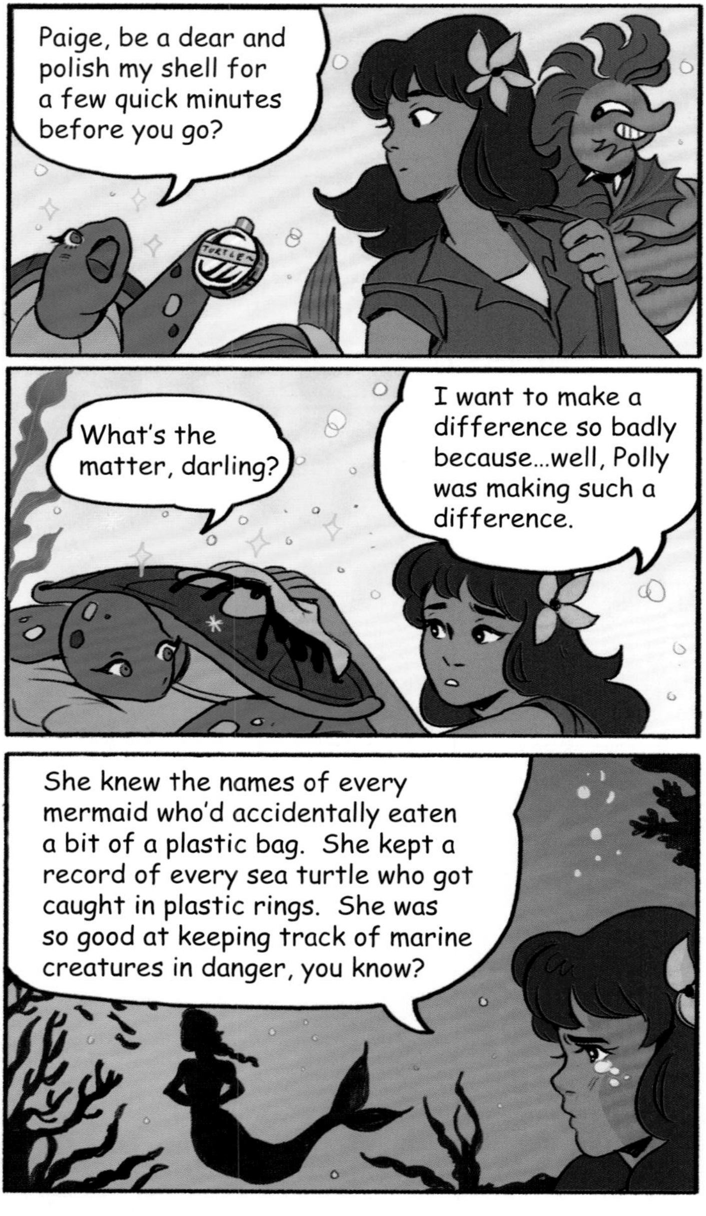
Paige, be a dear and polish my shell for a few quick minutes before you go?
TURTLE
What's the matter, darling?
I want to make a difference so badly because...well, Polly was making such a difference.
She knew the names of every mermaid who'd accidentally eaten a bit of a plastic bag. She kept a record of every sea turtle who got caught in plastic rings. She was so good at keeping track of marine creatures in danger, you know?

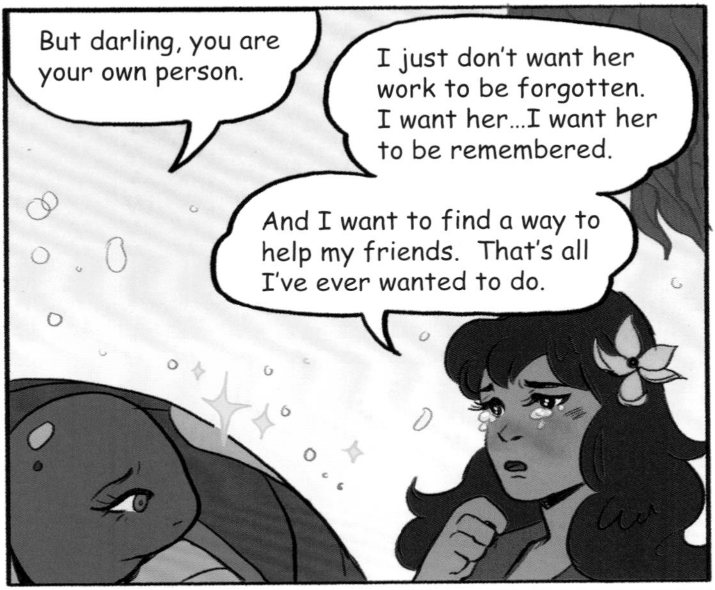
But darling, you are your own person.
I just don't want her work to be forgotten. I want her...I want her to be remembered.
And I want to find a way to help my friends. That's all I've ever wanted to do.

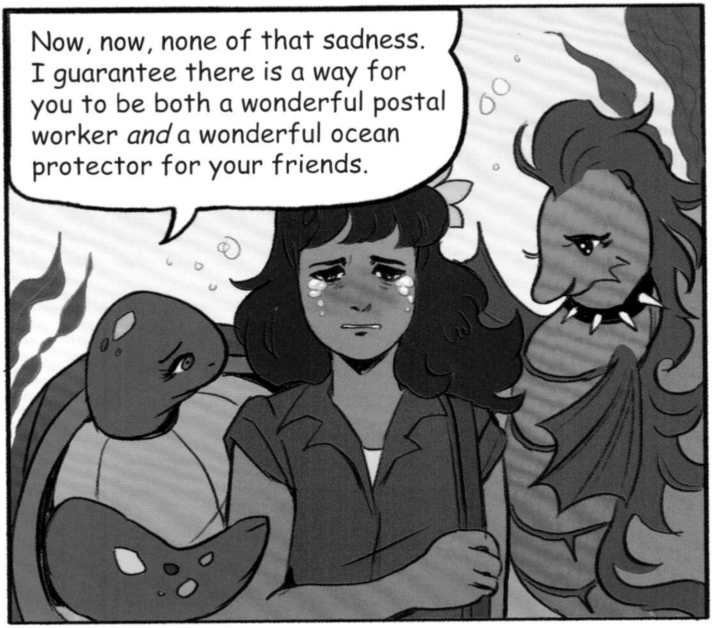
Now, now, none of that sadness. I guarantee there is a way for you to be both a wonderful postal worker *and* a wonderful ocean protector for your friends.

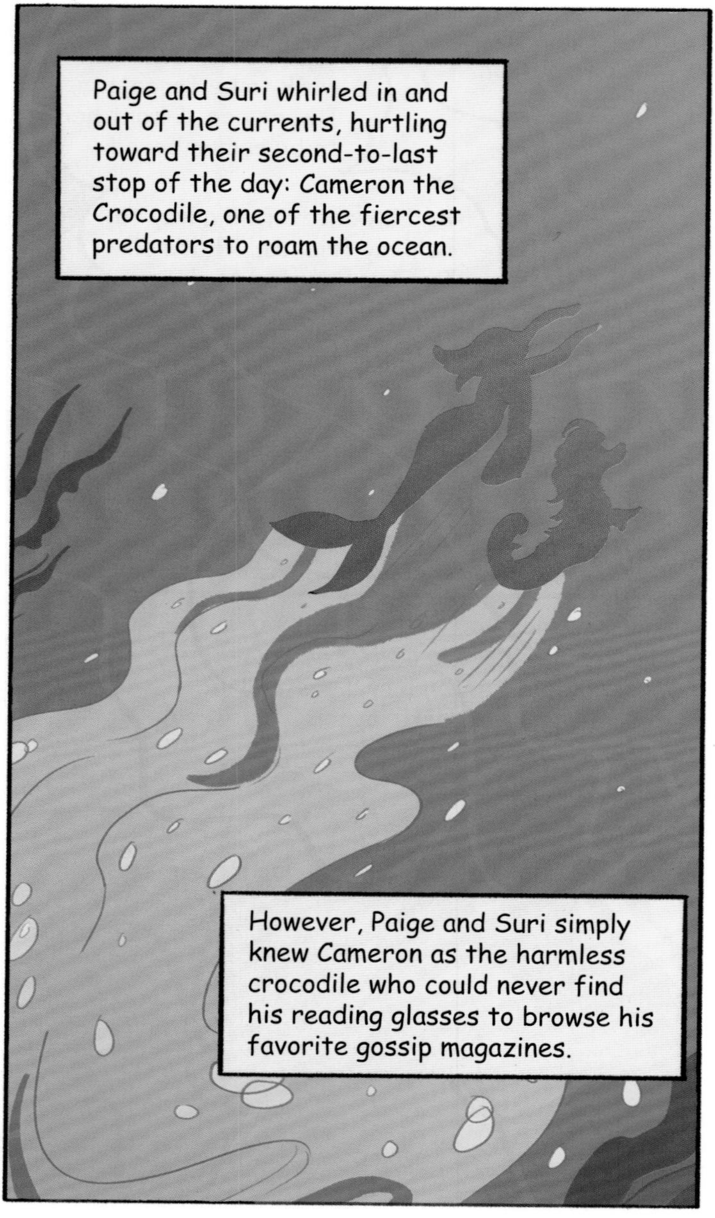
Paige and Suri whirled in and out of the currents, hurtling toward their second-to-last stop of the day: Cameron the Crocodile, one of the fiercest predators to roam the ocean.
However, Paige and Suri simply knew Cameron as the harmless crocodile who could never find his reading glasses to browse his favorite gossip magazines.

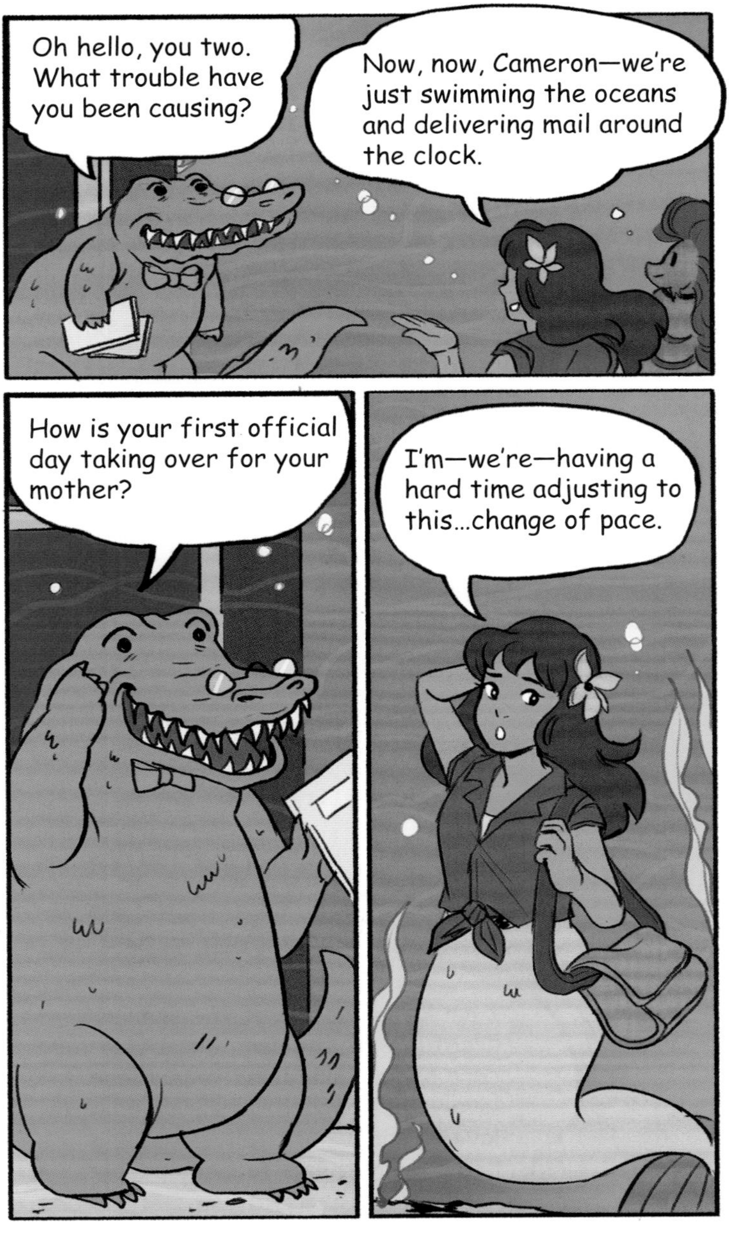
Oh hello, you two. What trouble have you been causing?
Now, now, Cameron—we're just swimming the oceans and delivering mail around the clock.
How is your first official day taking over for your mother?
I'm—we're—having a hard time adjusting to this...change of pace.

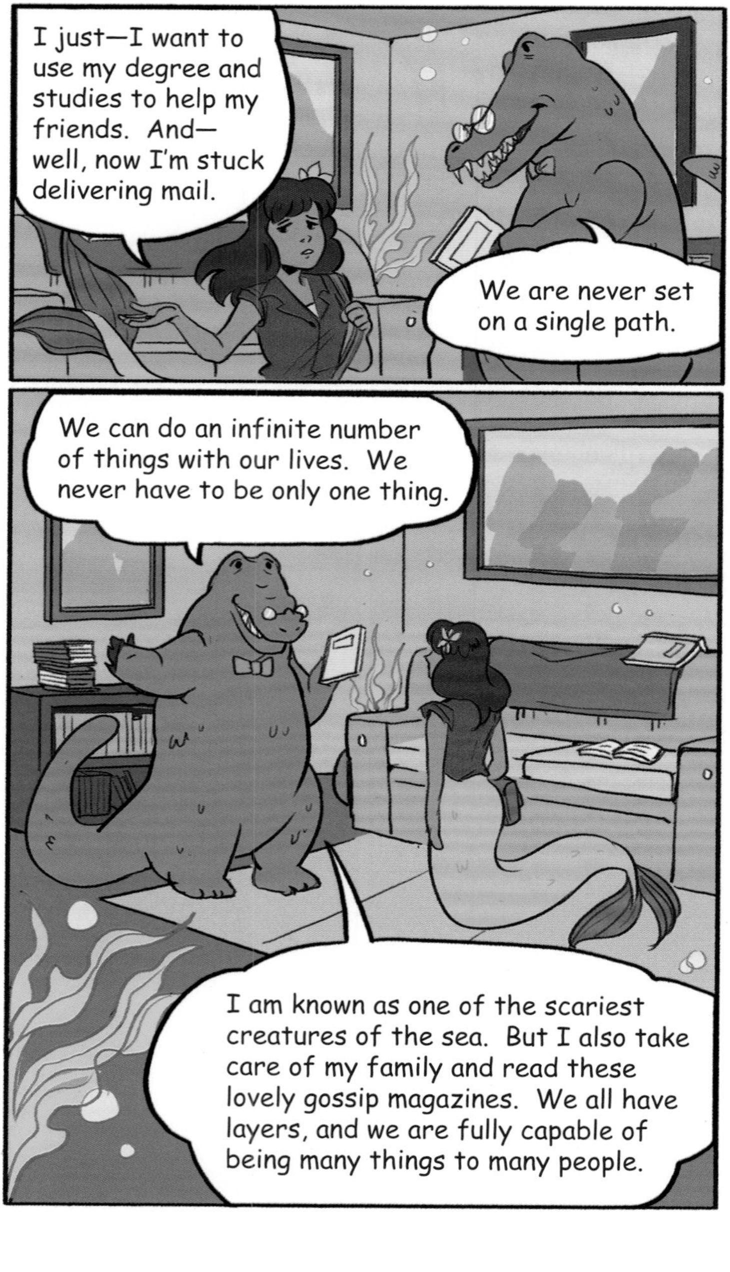
I just—I want to use my degree and studies to help my friends. And—well, now I'm stuck delivering mail.
We are never set on a single path.
We can do an infinite number of things with our lives. We never have to be only one thing.
I am known as one of the scariest creatures of the sea. But I also take care of my family and read these lovely gossip magazines. We all have layers, and we are fully capable of being many things to many people.

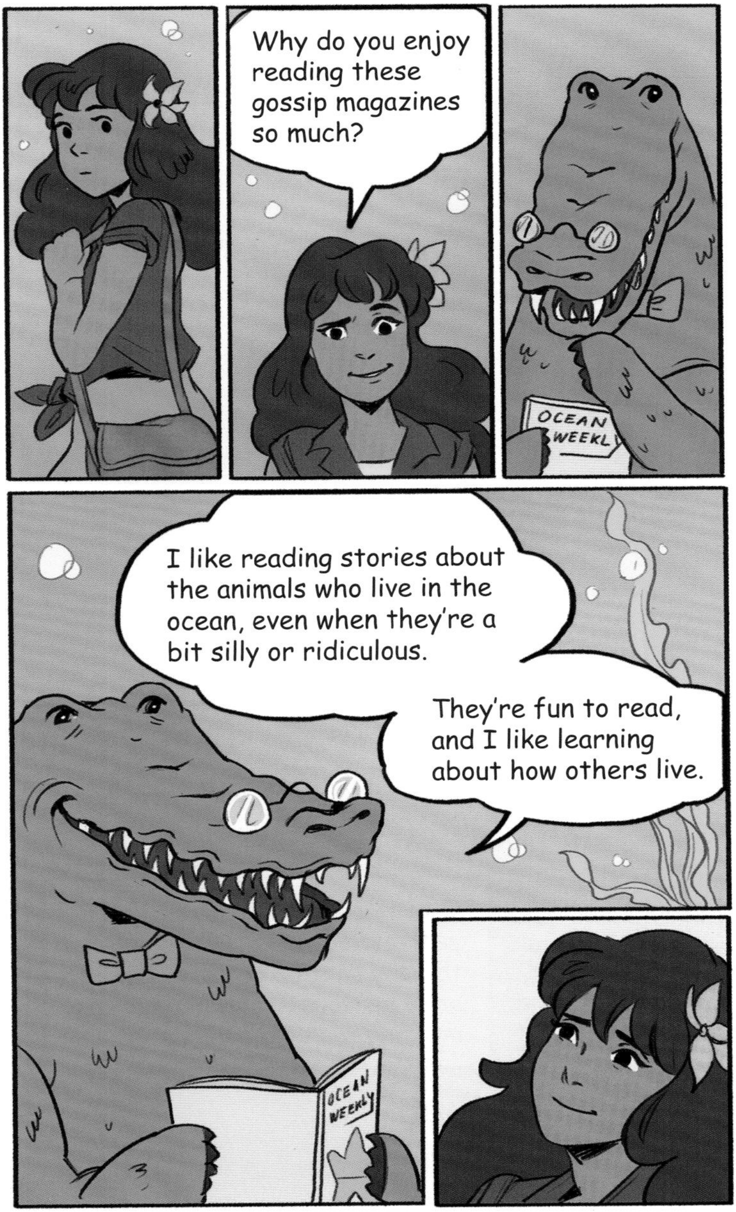
Why do you enjoy reading these gossip magazines so much?
OCEAN WEEKL
I like reading stories about the animals who live in the ocean, even when they're a bit silly or ridiculous.
They're fun to read, and I like learning about how others live.
OCEAN WEEKLY

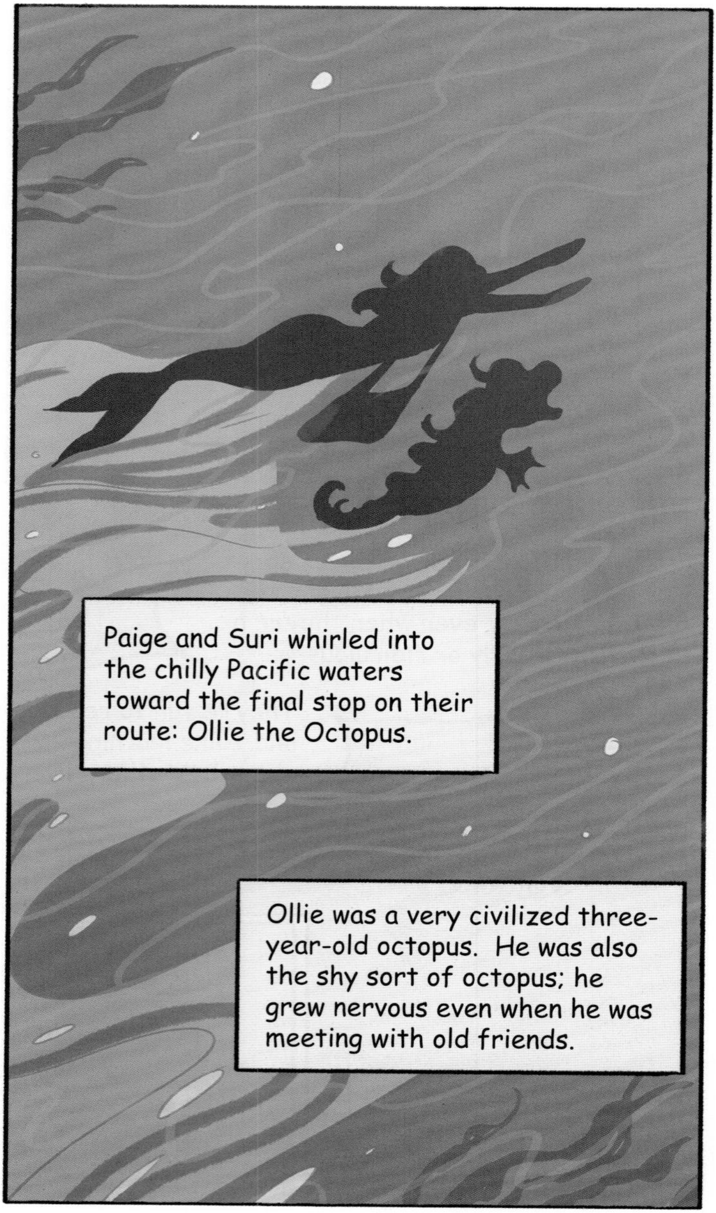
Paige and Suri whirled into the chilly Pacific waters toward the final stop on their route: Ollie the Octopus.
Ollie was a very civilized three-year-old octopus. He was also the shy sort of octopus; he grew nervous even when he was meeting with old friends.

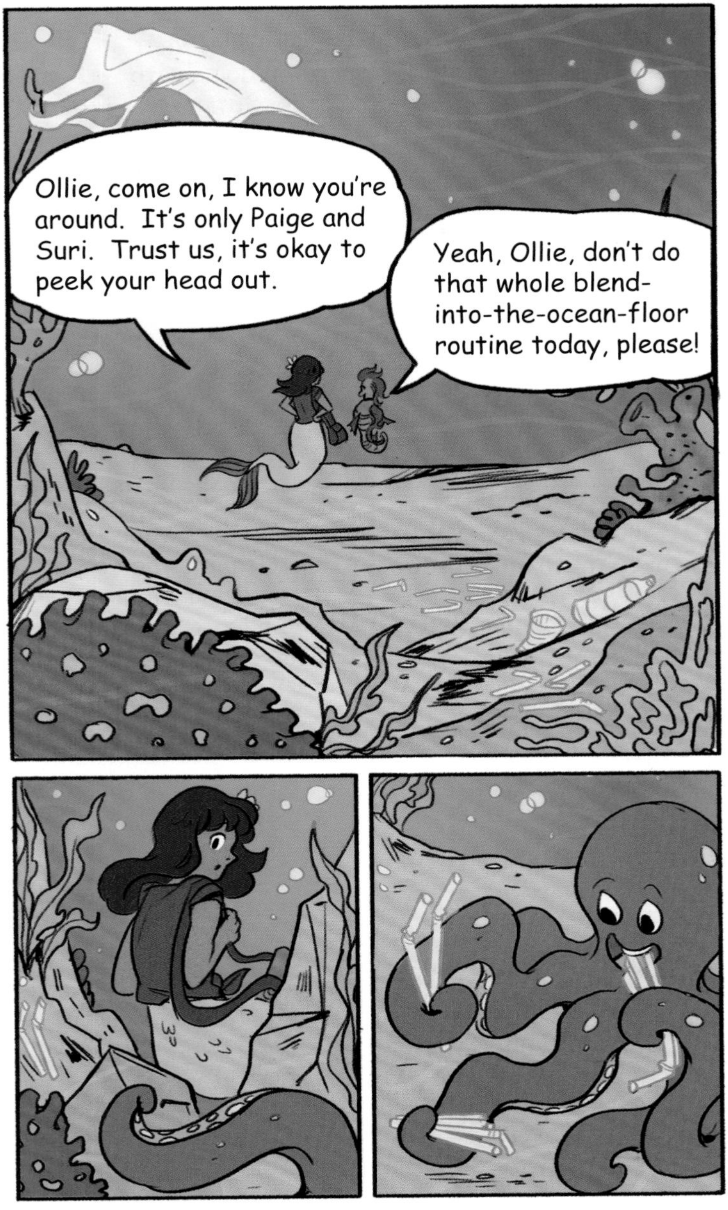
Ollie, come on, I know you're around. It's only Paige and Suri. Trust us, it's okay to peek your head out.
Yeah, Ollie, don't do that whole blend-into-the-ocean-floor routine today, please!

Oh no, Ollie, what are you doing with all those straws?!

Ollie, don't you ever, ever touch—or worse yet, eat—those straws! I don't want you to get hurt.

Sometimes when I am cleaning the ocean floor, I munch on the plastic I pick up. There's no need to get terribly worried.

No, this is exactly what I'm worried about! When Polly got sick, I promised her I would find a way to protect our friends from all the plastic around us.

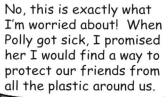

But...there's a lot of plastic around us, Paige—and we can only get rid of so much.

Polly used to say the most meaningful change has to come from above.

So, what exactly can we marine creatures do?

It's not about us.

It's about what the humans can do and how they can alter how they live their lives.

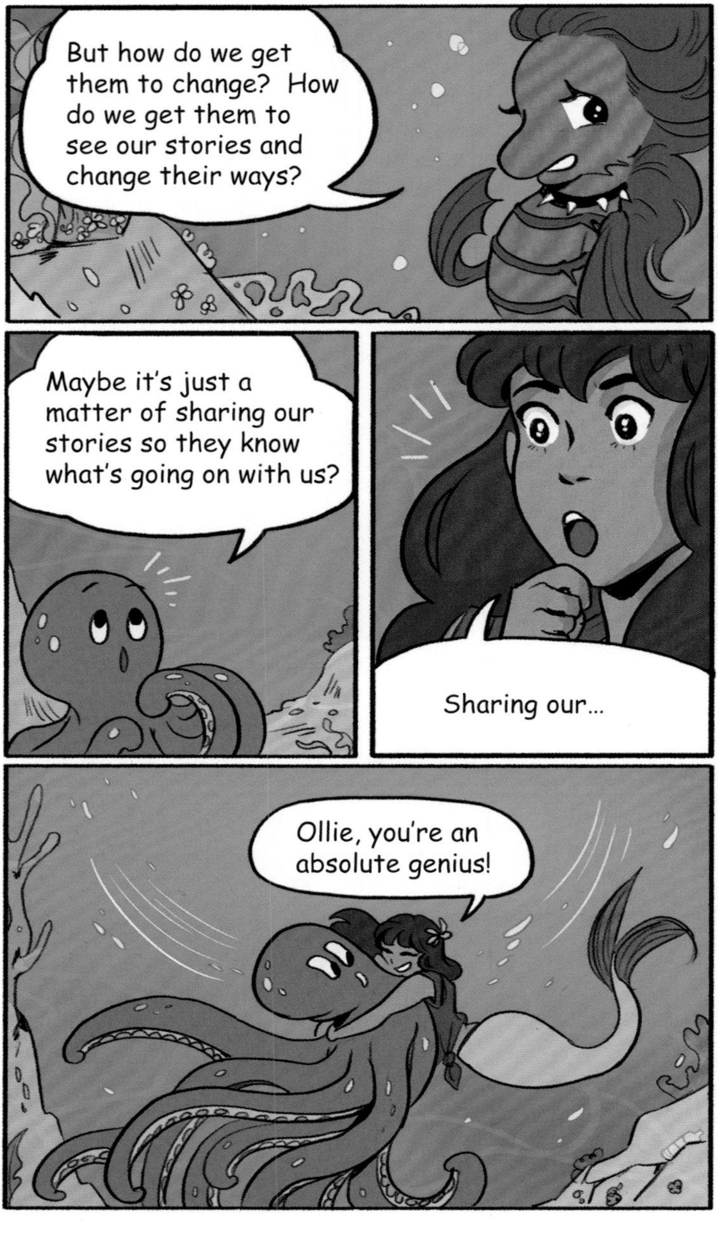
But how do we get them to change? How do we get them to see our stories and change their ways?
Maybe it's just a matter of sharing our stories so they know what's going on with us?
Sharing our...
Ollie, you're an absolute genius!

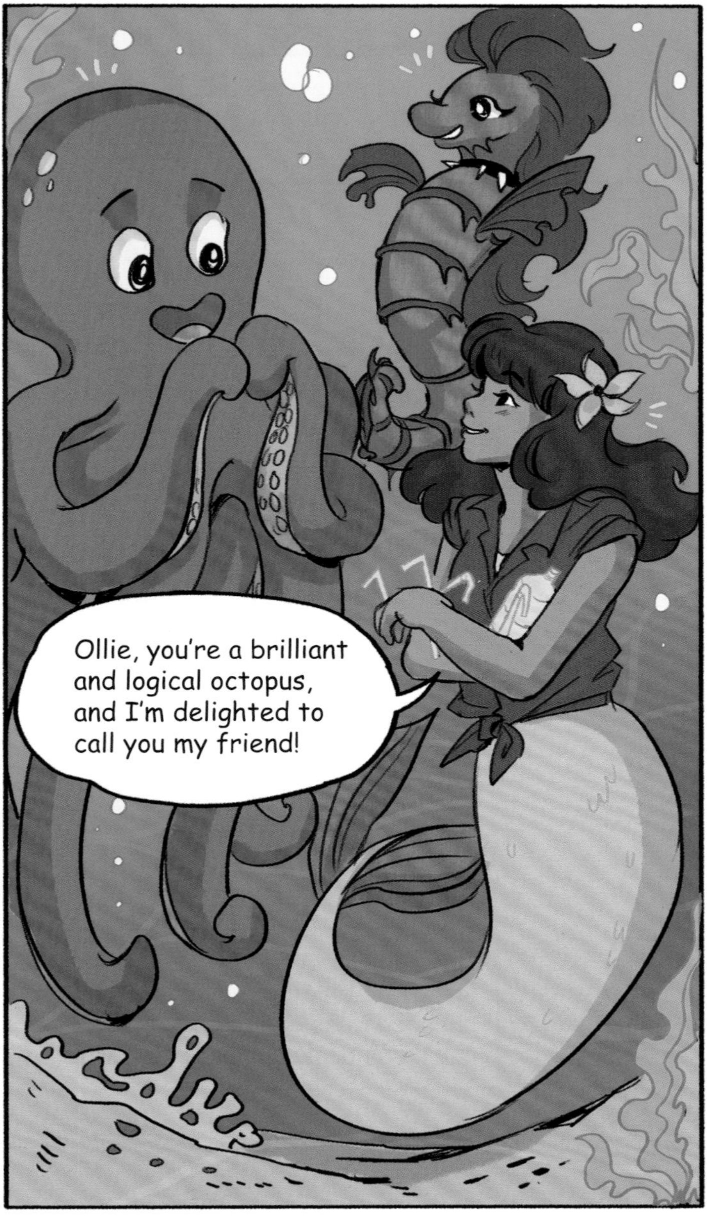
Ollie, you're a brilliant and logical octopus, and I'm delighted to call you my friend!

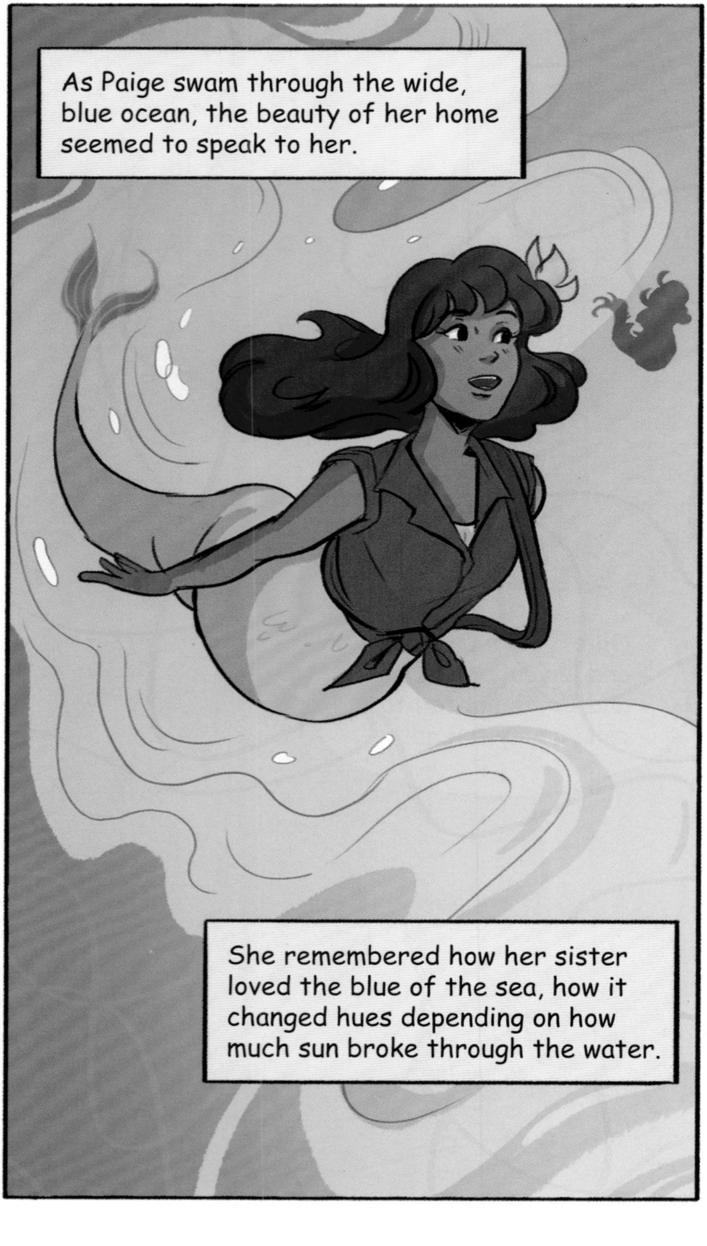
As Paige swam through the wide, blue ocean, the beauty of her home seemed to speak to her.
She remembered how her sister loved the blue of the sea, how it changed hues depending on how much sun broke through the water.

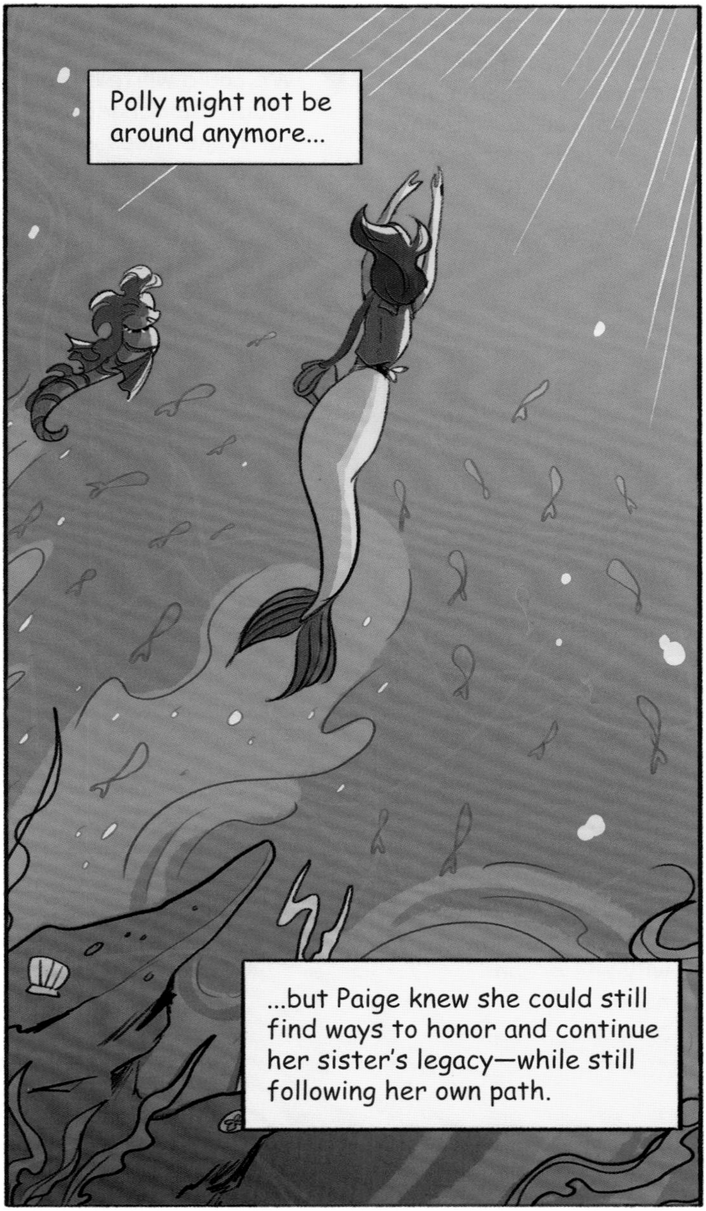
Polly might not be
around anymore...
...but Paige knew she could still
find ways to honor and continue
her sister's legacy—while still
following her own path.

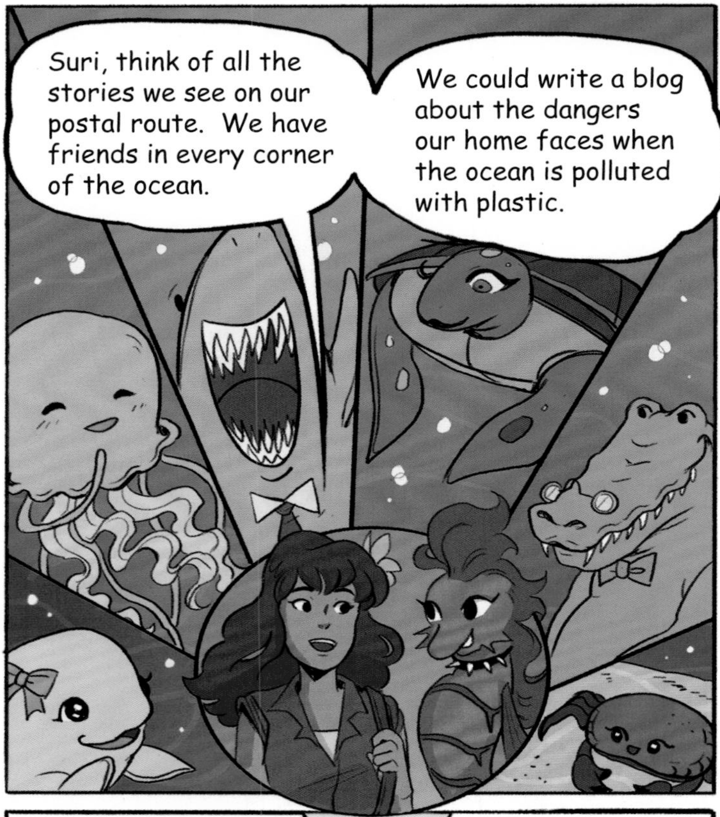
Suri, think of all the stories we see on our postal route. We have friends in every corner of the ocean.
We could write a blog about the dangers our home faces when the ocean is polluted with plastic.

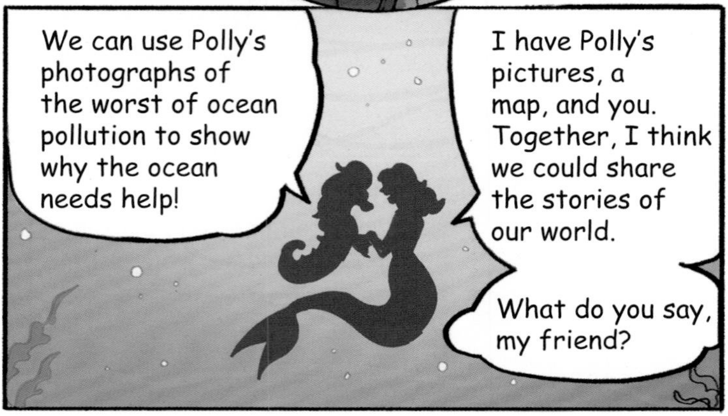
We can use Polly's photographs of the worst of ocean pollution to show why the ocean needs help!
I have Polly's pictures, a map, and you. Together, I think we could share the stories of our world.
What do you say, my friend?

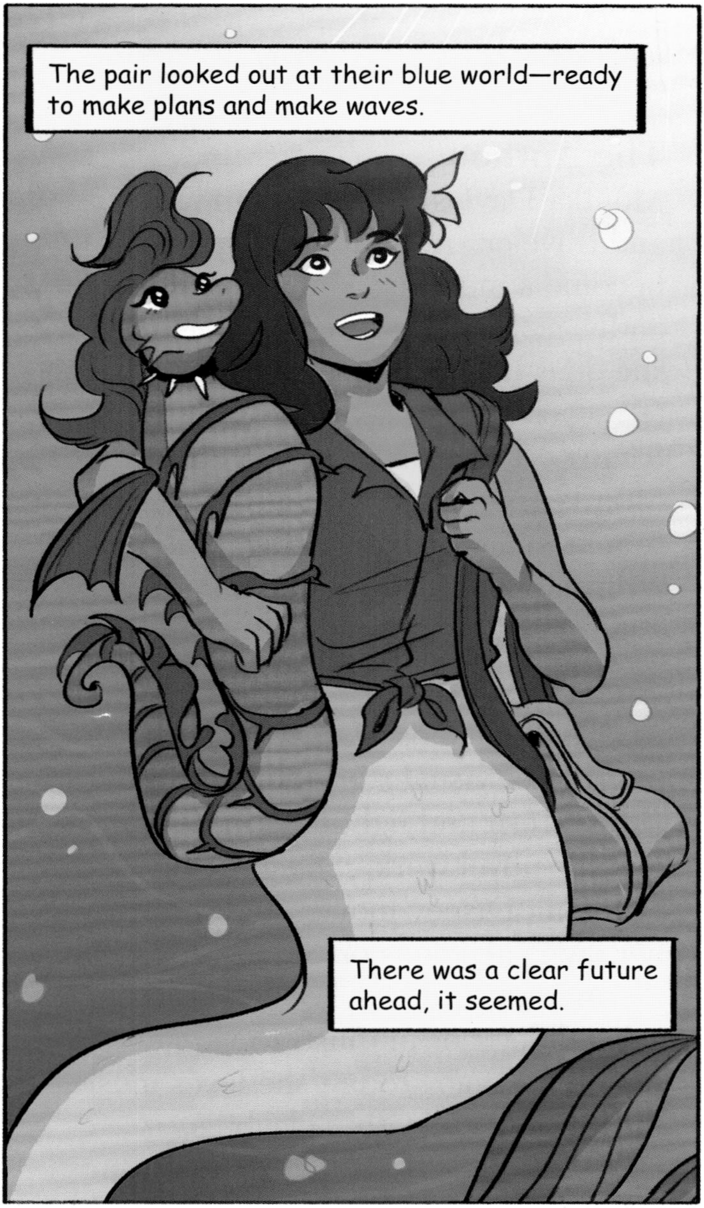
The pair looked out at their blue world—ready to make plans and make waves.
There was a clear future ahead, it seemed.

About Us

The Author

Monika Davies is a Canadian writer and traveler. As a kid, she wanted to become a mermaid—or a postal worker. Sadly, neither dream came true. But she does believe humans can take care to recycle as well as use less plastic. Saving our oceans is a team effort! Monika graduated with a bachelor of fine arts in creative writing. She has written over 20 books for young readers.

The Illustrator

Arielle Jovellanos is an artist with a passion for visual storytelling. She uses a fresh and light tone in her graphic novel work. She grew up watching Disney movies and drawing her own variations on Sailor Moon in the margins of her schoolbooks. She earned degrees in illustration and fiction writing. Today, she loves musical theatre and collecting playbills.